The Misadventures of Chair Head Boy

Written by Jace Shoemaker-Galloway

Illustrated by Merle Forman

Based on an actual event - sort of.
The inspiration for this book
came from an incident
at a local elementary school
although the story may be
greatly exaggerated!

DEDICATION

A special thanks to the children of
Lincoln Elementary School
who were the inspiration for this book.
To my mom, Merle Forman, the most creative
and talented person I know,
who brought my story to life
through pictures.
And to my children, Brandon and Janae,
and Elias and Christian.
You are my heart.

Little Elroy Langworthy
walks to school every day.
And misadventures follow him
all along the way.

Every morning Elroy searches for a hairy spider.
He surprises Mama when he plops it
down beside her.

Every week he hunts for insects
with his T-ball team.
Elroy loves to take the bugs
to make his sister scream!

In Miss Lulu's art class
he shoved crayons up his nose.
During morning recess
Elroy super-glued his toes!

Yesterday he spray-painted his bright red hair
pure white.
Giving the old principal
an unexpected fright!

During last week's school trip,
he freed the farmer's goose.
Opening the rusty gate,
he let that big bird loose.

Little Elroy is a rascal. That much we all know.
But no one quite expected
what he did two weeks ago.

Mrs. Helen Melon is a teacher
at Grant School.
All her first-grade students think
that she is really cool.

Everyone in class was getting ready
for the day.
All the kids were working
except Elroy and Janae.

All at once, the children gasped and then
began to chatter.
Mrs. Melon turned around
to see what was the matter.

Little Elroy's swollen head
was stuck inside the chair.
Seeing his predicament, she rushed right over there!

"Remove that chair at once, Elroy!"
the frazzled teacher said.
"I'm trying but it's stuck too tight on top
of my big head!"

"Hurry up," the children said.
"We have no time to spare!
Mrs. Melon, please cut off that big old school chair!"

Elroy heard the children's cries,
and he began to worry.
Doing nothing wouldn't help so he began
to scurry.

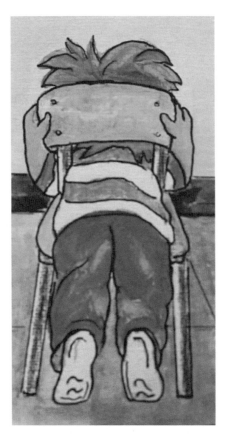

Little Elroy squirmed and turned.
The chair just would not budge.
Brandon, Grace, and Christian gave the
chair a great big nudge.

Little Elroy's hands and legs
were moving all about.
"Help me, please," he shouted.
"Help me get my head right out!"

The teacher tried to free his head
from that old school chair.
Twisting it and turning it, she even yanked his hair.

Pushing it and pulling it,
she tugged with all her might.
But his head was stuck inside
that chair just way too tight!

Regardless of their efforts and
despite their many tries,
"Now what do we do?" he asked
as tears flowed from his eyes.

So Elroy gathered all his strength –
he knew he had to fight.
And all at once he stood straight up and bolted
toward the light.

Like a superhero, Elroy hobbled to his feet –
zooming like a racecar
with his face against the seat.

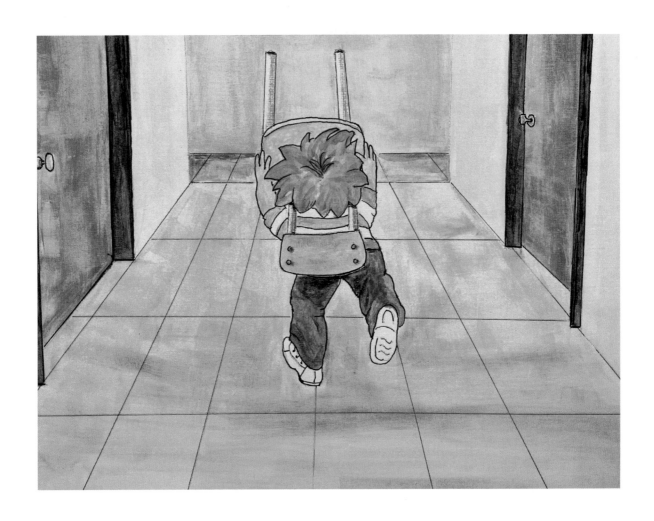

Out the door he ran and ran.
He sprinted down the halls...
being careful to avoid
the windows and the walls.

Dashing down the corridor,
he did not want to fall.
Little Elroy is not little –
now he's six feet tall!

Elroy found a secret room
and slammed the big door tight.
Sitting in the corner, Elroy slept that way
all night.

When he woke, he pulled and tugged and twisted
that old chair.
And just like that, it finally budged
and fell
from his red hair!

"I have learned my lesson,"
little Elroy finally said.
"Chairs are meant for sitting,
NOT to hold a person's head!"

Just in case you're wondering,
in case there is
some doubt...

KEEP YOUR HEAD OUT OF DESK CHAIRS
or it may not come out!

Due to Elroy's escapades,
there is a brand-new rule.
You don't EVER want to be
the Chair Head Kid
at school!

ABOUT THE AUTHOR

Jace Shoemaker-Galloway, a former freelance
writer and newspaper columnist,
had the wonderful opportunity of working with
children of all ages for 15 years.

As a former online safety educator,
Jace worked with hundreds of boys and girls
over the years and
thoroughly enjoyed
every single minute of it.

ABOUT THE ILLUSTRATOR

Merle Forman is a classically trained pianist
and talented artist
who enjoys a busy life out on the farm.

And oh...Merle just so happens to be the
author's mom!

The story - coming to life...

Little Elroy and the chair

Sketch of the goose & rusty gate

Made in the USA
Monee, IL
06 April 2022

94201779R00021